Noodle Lui Finds a Family

RONNIE BEATY

Fulton Books, Inc.
Meadville, PA

Published by Fulton Books 2020

ISBN 978-1-64654-913-9 (hardcover)
ISBN 978-1-64654-912-2 (digital)

This is dedicated to the one who brought us together—Becky Black

1

When Noodle was found, she was very sick!
Her skin was pink, and her fur was gone.

She was sent to the vet and then to a person to care for her until she found a home.

She felt very different from all the other dogs in the office because she looked like a piglet and not a pup.
She was sad and felt unwanted.

Finally, a family adopted her and took her home.
She was scared and excited.

9

She had a brother now. His name was Max and had shiny all-black fur. Her sister was Betsy, and she had all-white fur.

Noodle was embarrassed that she was hairless and pink. Sadly, she didn't feel like she belonged to the new family and was worried about being so different.

As time went on, she was getting better and noticed she was getting fur too.

Max and Betsy tried to play, but Noodle wasn't comfortable with them.

As time passed, Noodle's fur grew in.
It was time for a family picture.
She had never seen herself before but knew she was different
than everyone and wasn't looking forward to this.

Today is the day. *The picture was taken*!

Noodle looked at the photo, and a big smile came to her face!
She was all white with a black ear and a black eye.

She was a combination of all the family members!
This was the best day ever!

She finally felt like she fit in and was part of this family.
What a great day!
Now off to pull on Betsy's ears and start a good roughhousing.

About the Author

Ronnie has always loved animals. Being from Chicago and finally settling in Fort Worth, Texas, he now shares his modest home with Bob (Mr. Himself), Noodle Lui, Betsy Ross, and Maxwell P. Coltrain.

Enjoying working at Neiman Marcus for over fifteen years, he has made many friends and acquaintances. He loves the beach for vacation and has aspired to retire there someday, if Noodle approves of course.

Hoping this little story shows kids that being different is okay and we all deserve a "family" of our own, whether its related or selected.

It's important to have a sense of belonging, even if you are different. Enjoy this li'l tail.